This book is given with love

To: _____

From: _____

For all inquiries, please contact us at:
info@puppysmiles.org

To see more of our books, visit us at:
www.PuppyDogsAndIceCream.com

If I were your
Angel

Written by Dan Bright
Illustrated by Malgorzata Arska

If I were your angel, I'd use my wings...

to bring you so many wonderous things.

Borrow the moon's
beams of soft light...

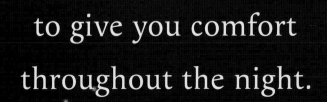

to give you comfort
throughout the night.

If I were your angel,
I'd use my hand...
To scoop up tiny
grains of sand.

Take that sand
down by the sea...
And build a castle
for you and me.

If I were your angel,

I'd use my feet...

To guide you up

and down the street.

Teach you how
to find your way...
So you are never
led astray.

If I were your angel,

I'd use my smile...

To bring you laughter

for a while.

Arrange the clouds,

so you can see...

How much happiness

you bring to me.

If I were your angel,
I'd use my cheeks...
To blow the wind
off mountain peaks.

Rustle the trees to
dance in place...
So leaves drift past
your smiling face.

If I were your angel,
I'd use my nose...
To find the sweetest
smelling rose.

Plant that rose beside

your room...

To care for it

and watch it bloom.

If I were your angel,

I'd use my ears...

to listen for your

falling tears.

Whisper softly
words of hope...
to ease the pain
with which you cope.

If I were your angel,

I'd use my harp...

To strum you notes

both flat and sharp.

Fill your ears
with joyful song...
So you can clap
and sing along.

If I were your angel,

I'd use my mind...

To free your thoughts

when you're confined.

Remind you what
the world can bring...
The falling leaves
and reborn spring.

If I were your angel,
I'd use my heart...
To lift you up
when we're apart.

Light your way
when there's no sun...
And provide a path
where there was none.

If I were your angel,
I'd use my eyes...
To watch over you
from the skies.

Marvel at
how much you've grown,
and how much you've
become your own.